Dear Parent,

Thank you for investing your valuable family time in reading about our adventures in the Roo World. This series was designed to teach children that their actions have consequences. That is why our phrase "Think it through... Do the Roo" was developed. We all need to think before we act, and children especially need to understand that they are responsible for their behavior.

The concepts of safety, self esteem and respect are presented as additions to your vital nurturing. Keep in mind, these are only suggestions to give you guidance. Your family should determine what works best for you.

Children grow up so fast. We want them to be happy, but we need them to be safe.

Please, make safety "roo-teen".

Your roo-pal,
Pati Myers Gross

**For my two joeys, Michael and Steve,
and Papa Roo, Dave.**

The Roo World Safety Seal

Fire Safety is dedicated to all the men and women firefighters who risk their lives every day to keep us safe.

Thank you to Anne Kymalainen and Michelle Foronda of the St. Petersburg Fire & Rescue Prevention Division for their expert assistance.

I also appreciate the St. Petersburg Police Department for the valuable training, guidance and support I have always received.

I would like to recognize a few of the many people who always encouraged me and believed in the Roo World concept: My husband, David, and children Michael and Steve; Edward, Barbara, Miller, and Michelle Myers; the entire Myers and Gross families; Lisa Smajovits; Sgt. Jeffrey A. Rink, Youth Resources Section, St. Petersburg Police Department; and a special thanks to George and Estelle Rosenfield.

Fire Safety
by Pati Myers Gross

**Author, Creator & Designer of Adventures in the Roo World: Pati Myers Gross.
Illustrator: Tom Gibson.
Artwork Consultant: Kathy Blue.
Editor: Carol Marger.**

Adventures in the Roo World © Young Roo Series © Volume II "Fire Safety"
Published By
Roo Publications, St. Petersburg, Florida 33707

Even though a fire can start out low,

Once it gets started, it loves to grow.

At first it burns tiny just like a mouse,

But fire can grow to the size of a house.

Its hot flames are quick; they burn and they dash,

And soon everything touched will turn to ash.

Fire will find you,
        so don't hide or stay;
When smoke is nearby,
        you must get away!

Never go back for your games or your toys;

A fire's not safe for girls or for boys.

Stop at the door first, and if it's hot to the touch,

Don't go out that way, the heat might be too much.

But if the door feels cool to the touch of your hand,
Go out this way, just as you planned.

If your clothes
catch on fire,
don't stand there
and pout,

It's Stop, Drop, and Roll,
that puts the fire out.

You can crawl out a window to safety outside,
You'll see loving people with arms open wide.

You need to get out quick;
fire's fast you know.

Don't try to fight a fire on your own;
Call for help from a neighbor's phone.

Smoke detectors in
every home is the golden rule,
Change the battery once a year to
use that handy tool.
Press the button once a month;
it's an important test,
To be sure your detector's
working at its very best.

Practice escape routes through windows and doors,
Consider it one of your family's loving chores.

Plan a special place outside for everyone to meet,
In case your house ever burns, pick a spot away from the heat.

Remembering safety sense,
that is the key,
Then you'll be
a JuniorFirefighter,
just like me.

Runabout's thumb is up with great pride,
Because you have safety on your side.